The Bird from the Sea

The Bird from the Sea

Renée Karol Weiss
pictures by
Ed Young

THOMAS Y. CROWELL COMPANY • New York

Manufactured in the United States of America
L. C. Card 71-106581
ISBN 0-690-14407-5
(Lib. Ed. ISBN 0-690-14408-3)
1 2 3 4 5 6 7 8 9 10

The Bird from the Sea

DO YOU KNOW what the most beautiful bird in the world looks like? Well, when this bird sings, his wings are as blue as the sky, and his tail is as gold as the rays of the sun. But when he soars above the water, his wings spread out like a rainbow, and his body changes colors like a shadow on the sea.

Now one day a gamekeeper and his daughter Devi saw this bird as they were walking through the woods. Devi cried, "There's the sea bird!" And she ran to the foot of a sparkling poplar tree. "He's lost!"

"You lost the bird you see?" asked her father.

"No, no. It's the captain's sea bird," said Devi. "You know, the captain who lives by the sea. He whistles. And that bird comes flying. Out of the sky. And he lands. Right on top of the captain's turban."

"Oh, you mean it's a bird from the sea," said the gamekeeper. And he stopped to look. "My, oh, my, that's a pretty bird," he exclaimed. "In fact, that's the prettiest bird I've ever seen. And he's not lost because you just found him."

Quite suddenly he grabbed Devi by the hand and began to run. "He'll never be lost again. But we must get help. We are going to catch that bird for our zoo," he declared as they rushed to town. "You have found

perhaps the most beautiful bird in the whole world. And our town shall have him!"

The door was open, so straight into the mayor's office they dashed.

"Help, help," the gamekeeper burst out. "Devi saw him—down by the sea. He's up in our woods. He's like a flying rainbow. We must catch him at once or he'll get away."

They seemed quite alone in that room piled with books and papers until a voice called out, "You can't catch a rainbow. And I can't catch one word you're saying. So please calm yourself. Then fill out the papers. Mayors don't understand anyone until they fill out papers."

"What papers?" panted the gamekeeper. "Oh, sir, where are you? We haven't time. It's Devi's bird—the most beautiful bird in the whole world."

All at once, over the top of a stack of scrolls and papers, up popped the mayor. "Oh, it's a bird," he cried. "The most beautiful bird! But why didn't you say so? Just last night I dreamed of him."

"Really!" exclaimed the gamekeeper. "You dreamed of the blue bird with the golden tail?"

"Golden?" repeated the mayor. Then he thought a moment. "Hmmm, I was sure he was silver with speckles. However, it doesn't matter. If he's the most beautiful bird, he's obviously the one I dreamed about. I assure you I wouldn't have dreamed of dreaming of any other bird. I'm never mistaken. That's why I'm the mayor."

Before the gamekeeper could say another word, the mayor cried, "Call the citizens!" And he dashed about bonging bells and shouting orders.

Immediately guards and townspeople came running.

"Get your nets," the mayor commanded. "Bring your bags and your sieves, your crocks and your pans. Bring whatever you have! We must go forth to capture the most beautiful bird in the world."

No sooner said than done. In a matter of minutes the entire town had marched off to the woods.

Now through the leaves the sea bird could hear the people approaching. He was delighted. He thought they had come to watch him perform. So he twittered and tweeted and trilled. And from his great height he swooped and somersaulted, catching bugs and flies.

But little by little he noticed that no one was listening to his songs. What is more, no one was pleased by his tricks. Then he saw the bags

and nets, and people surrounding him on all sides.

At once his singing stopped. His games stopped. And his heart beat very fast.

Devi was watching him. The bird, she thought, he's frightened! And before she knew it, she had stepped out and whistled *"Whee-whee-a-whee"* just like the captain who lived by the sea.

Instantly there was a swoop and a flutter and a streak in the air. When the crowd looked around, there was the bird, perched on Devi's shoulder.

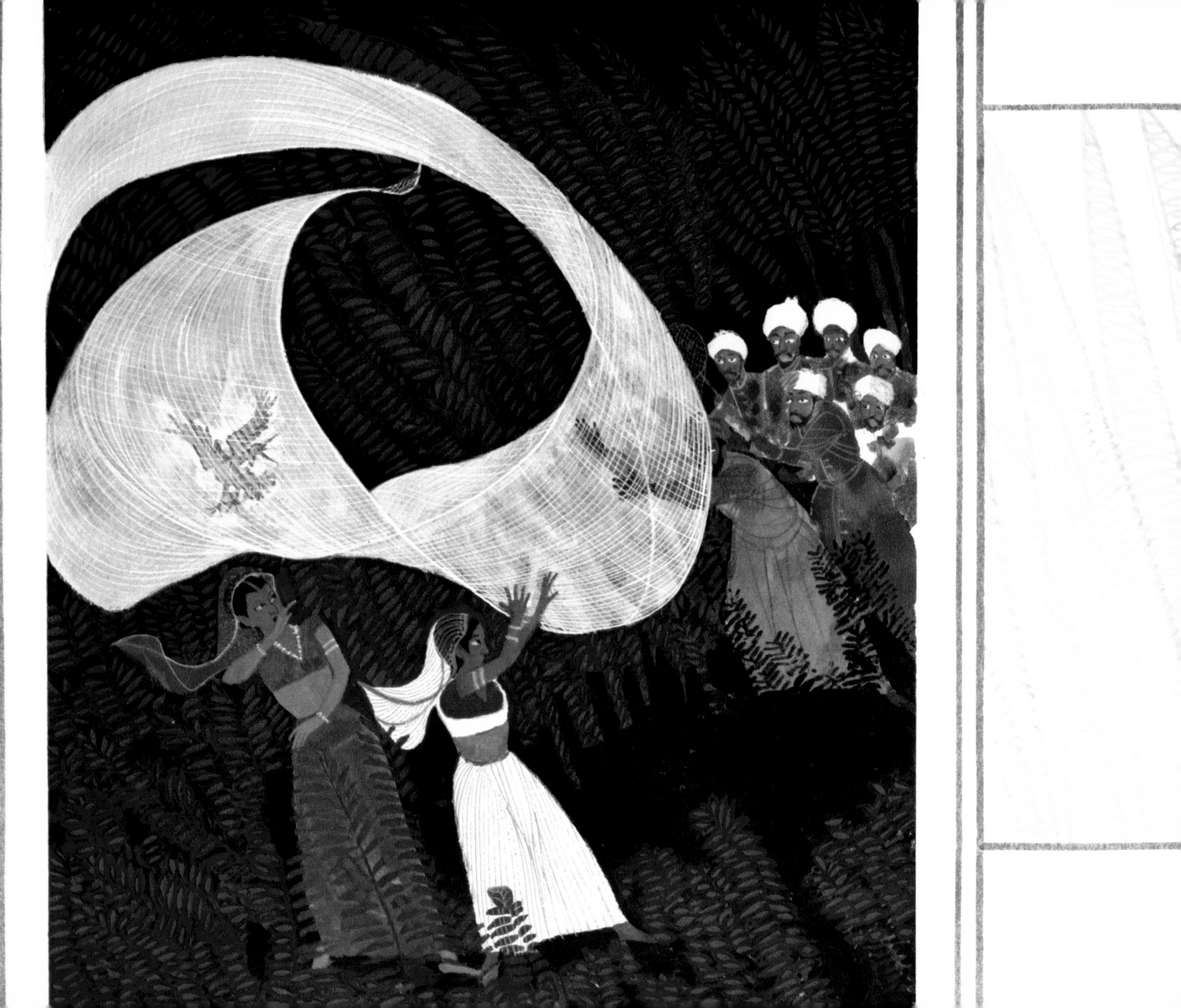

With the single toss of a net the bird was caught.

Devi hardly knew what had happened. But her heart was fluttering, too, and tears stood in her eyes.

"Hoorah!" shouted the mayor. "Devi has caught him." Then he looked closely at the bird. "I must say this is no ordinary 'most beautiful bird,'" he exclaimed. "Why, this must be the bird of good luck! Yes, yes. It's perfectly clear. Only good luck could be so beautiful. Dear me, this calls for a great celebration. We must tell the world that this bird has come to stay with us."

With that, the mayor pointed to the women. "I know what you'll do. You will cook three great feasts," he announced. Then he turned to the craftsmen. "You will make a magnificent cage." He turned to the children. "And you will provide entertainment. For tomorrow we must honor this bird as no bird has ever been honored before."

The mayor had spoken. The crowd rushed home to get ready.

The next day before dawn the whole town was buzzing. Children raced everywhere, their arms overflowing with flowers. In no time every wall, post, and pathway were blooming, and flowers even hung from the rooftops.

In the shops, meantime, the hammers of the craftsmen chimed and chattered.

And as for the women, it wasn't long before you could sniff out what they were up to. The smells of

spices and curries drifted through the flowery air, while crackling oils sizzled in the open pans. And even the walls of the mayor's kitchen seemed to bulge with baking as meal was sifted and nuts were crushed and honeyed sweets came from the ovens.

Many times during the day Devi ran to visit the bird. He was so quiet! "Wait till you see what we have for you," she would say. "You will be the happiest bird in the world."

Finally it was time. Crowds were lining the streets. The trumpeters stood up. *"Ta-ta-ta, da-da-da, ta-ta-da-ra,"* they tooted. "The children are ready to honor the bird."

The crowd held its breath as out of the woods and down those sweet-smelling paths danced the children. From head to toe they were garlanded with tiny orchids. And they were singing at the top of their lungs.

"The flowers are singing!" shouted the gamekeeper.

"Mm, mmm," said the mayor, nodding his head. "This is exactly the way children should honor a bird."

Immediately another *ta-ta-ta, da-da-da* sounded. The parade came to a standstill as two white horses appeared pulling a wagon with the bird of great beauty in his new cage.

"What a bird!" one man whispered.

"What a cage!" someone answered. "Why, that carpet is velvet. And the floor is inlaid with ivory. Look! There's a brocaded satin pillow, and a gold ceiling. And those bars are pure gold! Did you ever see such a cage to honor a bird?"

"It's the most beautiful cage in the world," shouted the mayor, "the only cage possibly possible for the most beautiful bird in the world."

When the carriage had passed, the crowd fell into step behind it and marched to the hall where the first banquet began. Great steaming curries were brought in, and honeyed fruits and sweets. From each dish the bird was given the first serving.

"I can tell you," said the mayor, "never was there such eating! Never such a parade or a cage or a party! Never were such honors paid to a bird."

So imagine how startled everyone

was when, in the middle of the banquet, someone screamed, "Father, O Father! Please call the mayor. Something terrible has happened! Something is the matter with the bird."

It was Devi. She had discovered that the bird had only pecked at his food.

At once the mayor rushed up. "What is it?" he cried as he looked at the bird. Then he sighed, "Tut, tut, Devi. This is nothing to scream about. The bird is just tired. A chase, a parade, and a feast are too much for one little bird. We will let him have a good rest, and you'll see. Tomorrow he'll twitter and tweet—and eat as much as any of us."

The bird looked up. Devi wiped her eyes. Everyone was happy again.

The next evening came. Bells tinkled. The air was filled with the hum of stringed instruments. And the bird sat in his cage at the head of the table. But he hung his head through all that sweet music. And again he ate none of the food.

"The bird, the bird," cried Devi. "He still isn't eating."

"My word, I know what's the matter!" exclaimed the mayor, clapping his hand to his head. "Naturally! Sea birds eat fish. Why didn't we think of it? Oh, my dear friends, what would you do without me? You'll see. Tomorrow the bird will eat enough fish for three feasts."

So the following night all kinds of fish were served—in spices and herbs, poached, baked, and broiled. And for dessert a sweet was brought in that was shaped like a fishbowl and gleamed with waves and sparkling fish.

But do you think the bird touched the fish or the sweet? Oh, no! In fact, by the end of the evening he was huddled sadly against the bars of the splendid cage, his head hidden under a wing. He was shivering and very thin.

"Oh, the poor bird," cried Devi.

Now even the gamekeeper was very upset.

"Stop the celebration," ordered the mayor. "Plainly something is the matter. But don't be alarmed. We will certainly cure him. Call the doctors. They'll know what to do for the bird."

"What has happened?" people asked as the doctors—three long-bearded gentlemen—strode through the crowd.

Now the first doctor bent to examine the bird.

"Aha," he said solemnly as he listened to the bird's chest. "It's a rare illness, I can tell you. If it stops the heart, it will stop it dead." But then he stood up and smiled. "However, don't worry." He tapped his black bag. "Here I have all kinds of pills I will give him. In a few days we will know. You see, if the bird lives, one of my pills will definitely have cured him."

"What? A few days? We can't wait a few days," cried the mayor. "This is the bird of good luck. And good luck can't be ill luck for even a few days." He turned to the next doctor. "Of course you'll cure our bird."

The second gentleman peered at the bird's closed eyes. "Aho," he declared. "I see it clearly. Something unpleasant is at the bottom of this. But now that I'm here, I will meet with the bird three times a week. After the bird has seen me, his eyes will be opened. He will see his trouble. And once he sees it, he will see that it isn't whatever it is that he sees."

"Sees what?" asked the mayor.

"Oh, I don't understand. But whatever it is you're saying will also take time. And of that, I must tell you, we haven't any."

Finally the mayor called the third gentleman. "You are the last one," he said. "Surely you will heal our bird this very minute—if not sooner."

The third doctor paged through his big leather book. "Ahem," he began slowly, "if the life of a bird must come to an end." He paused and pulled at his beard. "And if it must come to an end somewhere." He looked up into the sky. "Then this might well be the very spot where the life of this bird must come to an end."

"Come to an end?" cried Devi.

"Come to an end?" repeated the mayor and the townspeople.

"But the captain . . . . We can call the captain!" It was Devi, tugging on the mayor's coattails. "He'll know what to do for the bird."

"Captain?" asked the mayor. "What captain?"

"The old man," answered the gamekeeper. "Devi told me about him. He lives by the sea. The bird used to come when he whistled and sit on his turban. He's an old sea captain."

"Sea captain?" repeated the mayor. "But I've already called on my wisest men. What can a sea captain tell us? Nevertheless—" The mayor stopped to scratch his ear. "When you think about it, what do we have to lose? My, it's a good thing I'm the mayor! Very well, bring the sea captain."

In no time at all the old sea captain was there. He greeted Devi. Then he looked at the mayor and the guests, and then at the food and the instruments. "I live near the sea," he said. "Without its sound and its smell my heart grows heavy. So please tell me quickly. What can I do for you?"

"It's the sea bird," cried Devi.

"Our beautiful bird," said the gamekeeper.

"We had a parade and feasts," explained the mayor, "but the bird wouldn't eat. Now he is sick. My wise doctors can't cure him. Do you, by any chance, know what to do for our bird?"

"You fed the bird all this fine food?" asked the captain.

Everyone nodded.

"When you visit the sea, would you eat bugs and seaweed and fresh worms?"

"What do you mean?" said the gamekeeper.

"We don't eat bugs and worms," said the mayor.

"You put the bird in a golden cage?" asked the captain.

"Of course," said the mayor. "Nothing is too good for our bird."

"You gave the bird all that you wished for yourself?" the captain asked quietly.

"Yes," replied the mayor. "But what difference does all this make? Please hurry! We are losing time. The bird may not live through the night, and you have not even looked at him."

At last the captain went hand in hand with Devi to the cage. The mayor opened the door. The bird lifted his head.

"Oh," said the old man, startled to see how small the bird had become. Devi picked it up gently and placed it in his two hands. "They do not understand," he said softly to the bird. "They never long to hear water swishing over sand. Nor do they know what it's like to soar on the changing winds and watch the shadows of clouds on a sparkling sea."

"Please," cried the mayor. "What are you saying? Can you help our bird?"

The captain took the bird to the light. He shook his head thoughtfully. Then he looked at the mayor and the townspeople. "Do you really want me to heal the bird?" he asked.

"Naturally," said the mayor. "That's why we called you. And we're willing to pay you any price if only you cure our bird."

"Any price?" repeated the captain. "Very well."

He lifted his arms. There was a swoosh of wings. The bird rose into the air. He circled above the crowd. Everyone watched. Then, with a flutter, the bird flew straight out through the open doorway.

"What have you done?" cried the mayor.

"Our beautiful bird! Our good luck!" cried the townspeople. "We have lost it forever."

"I'm afraid it had to cost you the bird," said the captain. "For you see, that was my price for curing him."

The captain pulled his cloak over his shoulders and turned to leave.

For a long time the mayor sat and thought. His head went up and down, and back and forth. At last he shrugged his shoulders. "Ah, well," he sighed, "we have had a fine celebration. We have honored the bird as no bird has ever been honored before. And we shall always remember the parade and the cage and the feasts and the beautiful sea bird who came to visit us. Besides, it would not have been right to have kept good luck all to ourselves forever."

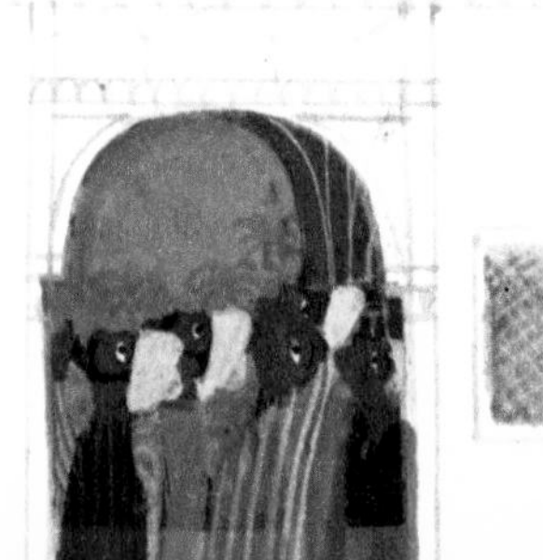

All at once the mayor jumped to his feet. "My word," he cried, clutching his head. "My papers! I must get back to my desk. I never filled out the papers. How will anyone know we entertained this great bird if I don't fill out the papers?" And with that he buttoned his coat, bowed to the crowd, and hurried away.

Soon, too, all the townspeople had left. Only Devi remained to wave to the captain as he disappeared down the long road.

Now, for the first time since the bird had been caught, Devi began to feel really happy. She could hear the ocean's mighty waves. The sun warmed her. She remembered the whistle call that brought the bird swooping in from the sea. And she thought of the sun shining on the bright plumes of the bird as he sat on top of the captain's turban.

ABOUT THE AUTHOR

Renée Karol Weiss is co-editor with her husband, Theodore Weiss, of *The Quarterly Review of Literature,* a magazine of contemporary creative writing. She has also worked as a teacher of small children and has played the violin in symphony orchestras and chamber music groups, including a touring string quartet which gave school concerts for children. She is the author of two other children's books: *To Win a Race* and *A Paper Zoo.* She and her husband live in Princeton, New Jersey.

ABOUT THE ARTIST

Ed Young was born in China and spent his childhood in Shanghai. When he came to the United States, he studied at the University of Illinois and at the Art Center School in Los Angeles. He lives in New York City. Mr. Young uses a different technique for each book, always based on careful research and a deep understanding of the theme to be expressed by both story and pictures. He has designed *The Bird from the Sea* to look as if the text were printed on embroidered oriental scrolls. His richly detailed illustrations were inspired by the Persian-influenced miniature paintings created in northern India during the elegant period of the Mughals.